In the Time Travel Secrets Series:

Moneyline Secrets
Family Secrets

Moneyline Secrets

by R.W. Wallace

Copyright © 2021 by R.W. Wallace

Cover by the author

Cover Illustration 408376694 © stokkete | depositphotos.com

Cover Illustration 11106798 © Hannamariah | depositphotos.com

All characters and events in this book, other than those clearly in the public domain, are fictitious and any resemblance to real persons, living or dead, is purely coincidental.

All rights reserved. No part of this publication may be reproduced, distributed, or transmitted in any form or by any means, including photocopying, recording, or other electronic or mechanical methods, without the prior written permission of the publisher, except in the case of brief quotations embodied in critical reviews and certain other noncommercial uses permitted by copyright law. For permission requests, write to the publisher, addressed "Attention: Permissions Coordinator," at the address below.

www.rwwallace.com

ISBN: [979-10-95707-81-3]

Main category—Fiction

Other category—Time Travel

First Edition

R.W. WALLACE

Author of the Ghost Detective Series

MONEYLINE SECRETS

A Time Travel Secrets Short Story

One

Gaëlle stared dumbfounded out the window of the Uber driving her from the airport in Las Vegas to the small town of Cave Creek. She had stepped out of the airport with her head still boggling at the idea of having slot machines in the arrivals area, only to be met with the driest heat she had ever had the displeasure of breathing. She had felt her throat and nose drying up almost immediately, and already regretted having made the choice not to bring moisturizer on this trip. She was only here for three days, which she had reasoned her skin should be able to take in exchange for a simpler trip through four airports. Except she could already feel her skin pulling at the corner of her eyes when she smiled—she was going to have to buy something once she was settled in her Bed

& Breakfast in Cave Creek or she'd spend all her mental energy on worrying about wrinkles and chapped lips.

Her focus needed to be on the goal of her trip.

Things had escalated so far between her mother and father at home, if Gaëlle didn't bring home proof that her mother was *not* a witch, she might have to bear witness to her father burning her mother at the stake.

Okay, he probably wouldn't actually do that.

But the events of the last couple of months forced her to add that "probably" in the sentence. And it scared the hell out of her.

Her mother claimed there was a perfectly normal explanation for the things she knew, but would never give it to neither her husband nor her daughter. She said she was sworn to secrecy and would keep her promise until the day she died.

In the past, whenever her parents had this fight, her mother would talk about her promise from "a long time ago." But in 2019, her mother vetoed a proposition to go on vacation in Australia because "half the country will go up in flames" and set off the biggest fight of all time when it actually happened months later. In the heat of the moment, her mother let slip a date.

"I may only have been eighteen, but I made a promise and I'll keep it!" she had screamed into her husband's angry, red face, ignoring his beefy fist under her nose and meeting his gaze without flinching.

Gaëlle's father hadn't reacted to the date—maybe he already knew and didn't care—but to Gaëlle, it was a clue that could help her find out what her mother's secret was. Something to save her parents' marriage. Make sure her mother was safe.

And solve the bloody mystery that had her resisting moving into her own place at twenty-three.

Her mother knew things that would happen in the future. Not everything, far from it, but things that made her father's accusations of her being a witch feel less far-fetched than they should.

She'd known France would win the World Cup against Croatia in 2018. The parents were planning their summer vacation and when Gaëlle's father proposed they borrow his brother's cabin in the Pyrenees for a week, and her mother had said, "But won't you want to watch the final? 1998 was a long time ago. It might not be as much fun to celebrate as when you were twenty-five, but it would be a shame to miss it because of bad reception."

She wouldn't tell anyone *how* she'd learned these things. But she had no problem sharing the information with her family to drive them crazy.

One time, when both parents had been out of a job for several months, she used the information to win some money. Gaëlle was only ten at the time and only remembered flashes, but they were all of her mother biting her nails to the quick, mumbling about ethics and Chamber of Commerce and *just once*.

She bet a large sum on a match between two American football teams and won enough to bide them over until Gaëlle's father found a new job.

She knew a lot of completely useless facts about American sports teams. Without knowing any of the rules of the sports, or showing any interest in the game other than confirming her predictions were right.

Once, she got a score wrong, but instead of being upset, she got super-excited and started buying history books by the dozens, frantically looking for "the split." Gaëlle still had no idea what she meant by that.

All the more reason for Gaëlle to get to the bottom of the mystery. Once a time frame was set, she had the element she needed. At eighteen, her mother had spent a year in the US as an exchange student. She had studied Art History at the university of Las Vegas.

And spent almost every weekend in the small town of Cave Creek, where her boyfriend lived. They met the first day of class and stayed inseparable from that moment onward—until her mother went back to Europe and never talked to or about the guy again.

Gaëlle got this information from her grandmother. And found her mother's stash of old letters from friends back in France in a cardboard box in the attic. It was frustrating learning about her mother's trip from an account three times removed—only her friend's responses to her mother's letters that clearly weren't giving much details either—but she found the one information she needed.

Whatever taught her mother all the weird facts she knew about the future was in Cave Creek. She didn't go anywhere else the whole year, because that's where Beau was.

Her mother had dated a man named "beautiful." Getting over *that* had taken a few giggling fits. She wondered if his looks fit his name.

If her mission went as planned, she might even find out.

After all, if he was with Gaëlle's mother every time she went to Cave Creek, he would also have done or seen whatever she did. He was the first point on Gaëlle's to-do list for the trip.

Gaëlle looked up Cave Creek online before getting on a plane, of course. It looked straight out of a Western, with saloons with swinging doors, a huge fancy hotel, and dry, wide roads like only the Americans know how to make.

What she *hadn't* found online, was what first met anyone driving into Cave Creek: Fast Food Row.

The driver supplied the name when he saw her gaping out the window. Fast food joint after fast food joint, as far as the eye could see. Not a single one missing. Against the backdrop of the beautiful Nevada desert with Las Vegas in its wide valley and the imposing mountain ranges in the background. The dichotomy was jarring.

Americans really were a weird bunch.

But not long after, they pulled into the town proper, and the picture-perfect Western appeared, exactly as promised. They drove past the Golden Dream Hotel that Gaëlle had salivated over when looking for a place to stay but eventually abandoned because it was way out of her price range.

The Wilted Horseshoe Bed & Breakfast a couple of minutes farther into the town and down a slightly narrower side street, was more budget friendly. Gaëlle paid the driver—probably tipping too much but being too scared to tip too little—and stepped into the hot afternoon.

Maybe she shouldn't have come in June. She could feel the hot air entering her lungs and a drop of sweat already making its way down her back inside her thin blouse.

No wonder the streets were deserted.

Pulling her old and battered carry-on suitcase behind her, Gaëlle stepped onto the wooden porch with the old-style sign showing a horseshoe that somehow managed to look wilted—hats off to the artist for that one—squeaking overhead, and entered the Bed & Breakfast.

Her eyes took a moment to adjust to the darkness inside. A tiny reception area the size of a school desk was the first thing to meet the eye. Behind it, an empty chair, and on the desk, a laptop that looked to have seen better days. To the left, in front of a window opening on the street, a worn leather lounge chair, with a worn leather man sleeping in it.

Only a slight exaggeration. The man's skin was tanned like he'd spent his entire life in the sun, gouged with wrinkles and laughing lines, and his worn cowboy hat, jeans, and cowboy boots generally added to the impression.

Gaëlle felt like she's traveled through time—and her TV. On some level, she had always thought these places and people only existed on the screen. Seeing a real-life person actually wearing a cowboy hat unironically just added to the off-kilter feeling of this entire trip.

Although he didn't look *bad* with a hat, surely he'd look better without it?

"Hello there, Ma'am," a gravelly voice said from the dark corner behind Gaëlle, making her jump and squeak in fright. "I assume you're Miss Germain?" He pronounced it "German" but Gaëlle didn't bother correcting him. She tried that at the airport in Florida and it only increased the confusion.

She turned to face the man belonging to the voice. "Yes, I am—"

Oh. Hello.

Fine, so some men could look good in cowboy hats. Possibly more than good, if Gaëlle's galloping heartbeat was anything to go by.

The guy was almost a head taller than Gaëlle—which said more about her than about him—and stared at her with a pair of green eyes so piercing it felt like they must be emitting light from beneath the relative shade of his hat. He had a wide mouth showing off white but slightly crooked teeth, and a strong nose. Gaëlle had always been a sucker for a good nose.

He wore a simple, white t-shirt that highlighted his perfect tan, a pair of worn jeans stretching over muscular legs, and cowboy boots so well-worn they seemed to be part of his feet. It was like he'd been cut out of an old cigarette advert—minus the cigarette.

"You are…?" he prompted, a smile playing on his lips.

"Miss Germain." Gaëlle finally found her voice.

"Welcome to Cave Creek, Miss. I'm Eli. I hope your visit with us will be pleasant."

Gaëlle was guessing "weird" or "informative" would be closer to the truth. But with another glance at the man's strong profile, she admitted she wouldn't mind adding "pleasant" to the list.

Two

AFTER A QUICK shower and a change out of the clothes she had worn for her twenty hours of travel from France, Gaëlle exited her room to start her search for Beau. She was dead tired but didn't want to sleep. Jet lag was going to mess with her for her short stay anyway, and she hadn't come here to sleep. There would be time for that back home.

Eli seemed to be waiting for her at the front desk. He leaned against the doorjamb with one foot pulled up to rest against the wall—looking extremely cowboy-like. Did he do it on purpose or did people around here naturally behave like they were part of a film about the old West?

"My dad will watch the place for the rest of the day," Eli said with a nod toward the old man still sleeping in his chair. "Would you care for some company as you explore our little town? Was the room to your liking?"

Was it odd for him to offer to be her babysitter? Or was he just being polite? Was she supposed to say thanks, but no thanks? Gaëlle was a little too tired to tackle the nuances of the cultural gap, so decided to simply do what would help her the most in her quest.

"I wouldn't mind some company," she said with what she hoped was a graceful smile. "I'm looking for information about someone named Beau. He used to live here in the early nineties. I don't suppose the name rings a bell?"

Clearly, it did. And not in a good way.

Eli's easy smile fell and he straightened from his slouch, tipping his hat back a little so his gaze increased in intensity.

"Beau is a fairly common name," he said slowly. "And we've had our fair share of them over the years. There's one living down by the golf course right now. But he only moved here four years ago."

Gaëlle wondered if perhaps she should have had that nap after all. When she was tired, her filter tended to come off, which meant she risked telling the man too much too soon. Or make a complete fool out of herself. And she didn't have the mental capacity to think through all the possible explanations for why the mere mention of Beau's name would garner such a strong reaction.

Finesse was out of the question. Direct tended to work best anyway. "I'm interested in the one who lived here in 1993. The one that made you go all dark and stormy right now."

Eli opened his mouth, probably to object to the description, then closed it again. His gaze hadn't left Gaëlle since she came into the room and now it turned speculative. "Did you have a destination in mind for searching for this person?"

Gaëlle shrugged. "Figured I'd ask around until I found someone who knew him. Which I did." She offered a sweet smile, the one that always made her father narrow his eyes in suspicion. "Tell me, Eli, where should I go to get information on this Beau who lived here in the nineties?"

In the silence that followed, Gaëlle didn't break eye-contact. She became very aware of the sound of the air-conditioning somewhere behind her and the buzzing of a fly circling the old man in the chair. She hoped he wasn't dead.

Finally, Eli let out a long breath and rocked back on his heels. "I guess I'd be as good a person as any to tell you about him. But not here. How about we walk down to the saloon two doors down, and we can discuss Beau over a drink?"

An actual saloon. What was the difference between a saloon and a bar, anyway? Or a diner? Dive bar? So many words for a place to find sustenance.

And some sugar would be great just about now, to get her brain back on track.

"That sounds lovely," she said. "As long as they have drinks without alcohol?"

"'Course they do, Miss." And he tipped his hat and held the door for her.

Two minutes of walking in the insufferable heat and Gaëlle started to see the appeal of a cowboy hat. At least Eli's face was in the shade. As they stepped through the doors of the saloon and were hit with the blessedly cool inside air, she asked, of nobody in particular, "Are women allowed to wear cowboy hats? Do they make them in pink, or with sparkly decorations or something?"

Eli didn't say anything, but his face clearly answered. And it was *no*.

Gaëlle huffed. If she wanted a cowboy hat, she'd get a cowboy hat.

Right after refreshments.

She was in a *saloon*. How exciting.

It wasn't all that different from a bar back home, with a long bar and high stools along one side and a handful of tables on the other. An underlying smell of beer and man, and some music playing in the background. Slightly sticky floors. Still, it had a definite Wild West feel to it, with dark wood and pictures of cowboys on the wall and— Was that the head of a cow on the wall?

Americans.

"What would you like to drink?" Eli asked as he slid onto the barstool at the very end of the bar. He removed his hat and set it carefully on the bar, revealing a full mop of dark hair, slightly mussed because of the hat.

Brain close to flatlining, Gaëlle went with a Coke. She didn't have the energy to figure out something new to try out. She wanted cold and she wanted sugar. Caffeine would be a nice bonus.

Eli was kind enough to wait for Gaëlle to finish half her drink, meaning some of her brain cells were back to functioning, before he started talking. "Tell me, Gail, how do you know about Beau? Is it okay if I call you Gail? I saw it on the reservation."

"It's Ga-ëlle." Gaëlle pronounced it several times for him, stretching each syllable.

Eli shook his head. "See, I hear the first part. 'Ga.' That's fine and dandy. But the second part? It just sounds like you're about to puke."

Not sure if she should be amused or offended, Gaëlle shook her head. "Let's just go with Gail, then."

"Thank you kindly. Now, how'd you know about Beau?"

Gaëlle was supposed to be the one to ask the questions, but it probably wouldn't hurt to answer some of his first, as a show of good faith. "My mother knew him when she stayed in Las Vegas in 1993."

"And why are you looking for him now? Does you mother know you're here?"

"I'm twenty-three years old. I don't need my mother's permission to go on a trip."

"So, no. You mother doesn't know. I'm guessing she would have told you not to come if you'd asked her."

This guy was getting annoying. "So you not only know Beau, but also my mother?" She pushed her empty glass away and glared into Eli's eyes, ignoring all thoughts of beautiful and green in favor of anger. "Why don't you just tell me where I can find Beau, and I'll ask him my questions directly."

"Beau's gone. Nobody's seen him since 1995."

"Oh." Gaëlle quite literally deflated. Ran a hand over her face and signaled the bartender for another Coke. "What happened?"

"Nobody knows. Beau is one of the many weird stories surrounding Cave Creek, though he's one of the more spectacular."

Gaëlle shook her head. "Fine. I'll bite. What happened?"

Flashing a stunning grin, Eli ordered another beer and settled in to tell the story.

Three

Beau was the son of one of the oddest men in Cave Creek. Beau had always been outgoing and helpful, kind to everyone no matter who they were or where they came from. His father was something of a recluse and a mystery, often going away on "business trips," and coming back with suitcases full of money. He never tried to hide it, and always went straight from the airport to the bank, depositing everything but a couple hundred dollars. "For my sweet tooth," he'd always say. Then he'd go back to his home and mostly stay there, alone, until he ran out of money and off he went on his next trip.

When the town started to gossip, the sheriff made an investigation. Even though Beau's dad did his business out of town, nobody wanted a criminal living among them, being treated like any upstanding citizen.

But he never found anything illegal, only the man going to various sports games and winning big on betting against the favorites.

Always winning big.

Which was suspicious, of course, but nobody ever managed to prove the man did anything illegal. He didn't have the network or influence to rig any games, nor, frankly, the brains.

People finally came to accept this as normal, just one of the many weird things happening in the small town. Especially once the old man got into the habit of donating half of everything he won to local charities, the school, or the Historical Center.

Then he died in 1994, and left everything to Beau.

Who took up his father's habit of betting on sports games. But not in various cities around the country. He stayed closer to home, and made all his bets through the same bookmaker in Vegas. It was easier, he said, and why should he have to hide what he did when he wasn't doing anything illegal?

When he won *every* bet, it quite naturally drew the attention of law enforcement.

Who cornered Beau in his house one day, search warrant in hand.

Beau, who had been increasingly excluded from social activities as everyone became convinced he was up to no good, had somehow managed to make his house into a fort. He'd boarded up all the windows, as well as the front door.

The sheriff finally made his way inside through a window on

the second floor. But when he searched the house, he found no trace of Beau.

Onlookers had seen Beau through a window when the sheriff first knocked. Despite the house being surrounded, nobody had seen him leave.

He simply disappeared.

It was one of the Cave Creek classics.

Four

Well, at least it would explain why Gaëlle's mom hadn't kept in touch with Beau. He disappeared only a year after they split up. Gaëlle wondered if her mom knew what happened.

The important thing here, though, was the betting on sports results. It might have seemed somewhat normal for a young American male to be interested in sports, but much less so for Gaëlle's French mom who couldn't tell a soccer ball from a rugby ball, much less a football.

"What happened to Beau's house?" she asked Eli when he paused to take a sip of his beer. "Is it still here?"

"It's still here, all right." Eli smacked his lips and a frown appeared between his brows. "When the sheriff gave up on finding the man or his information source, it was put up for auction. The Chamber of Commerce bought it."

"The—" Gaëlle's breath caught. "What does the Chamber of Commerce do? Did they want it to set up offices or something?"

Eli's sharp gaze was boring into Gaëlle. He didn't miss her rising excitement. "It's been standing empty ever since. I saw a group of Chamber of Commerce members go in once, carrying a heavy bag that looked to be filled with tools. They came back out several hours later, looking tired, but the kind that comes after a good day's work. Thought maybe they *were* going to use the building for something useful, but as far as I know, nobody's been back since."

He leaned closer and Gaëlle could smell the beer on his breath, mixed with something minty fresh. "Does the name mean something to *you*?"

Gaëlle hesitated. Could she trust this man? Would he help her or try to hinder her?

Would she really stand a chance at finding what she was looking for *without* him?

"My mom knows a lot of weird facts." Once she decided to tell him, she got it all out quickly. She kept her voice low so the bartender wouldn't overhear. "Like, she knew Australia was going to be ravaged by huge fires in 2019. A couple of other things along the same veins over the years. And she knows a lot of sports facts. Results of games and such. *Before* the games happen."

Eli lifted an eyebrow at this but didn't interrupt.

"My dad thinks she's a witch and she won't tell him how she knows all that stuff, so he gets more and more convinced. Unlike your Beau and his dad, though, my mom never used this information for her own gain—except once. And when she did, she mentioned the Chamber of Commerce. She was very worried."

"You're saying she stayed here with Beau? In his house?"

"I think so." Gaëlle tapped her fingers on the bar top. "Has nobody else lived in that house since then? Or even at the same time? What about the mother?"

Eli cleared his throat. "The mother disappeared when Beau was ten."

"Disappeared. Like Beau disappeared?"

"Yeah." The word comes out on a whoosh. "This was a while ago, obviously, but I seem to remember someone saying something about this being what made Beau's father retire from society and stay all alone at home, talking to nobody but his son and only leaving to earn money betting on games."

Something weird was going on in Cave Creek, all right. And her mother had been right in the middle of it.

"The way I see it," Gaëlle said, "we have two options. We either go talk to the Chamber of Commerce—who obviously knew what went on in that house and covered it up afterward—or we go scope out the house. I say we go with the house." If the Chamber of Commerce people had been silencing people for decades, there was no reason they would be forthcoming with any information.

Eli smirked and his pretty eyes sparkled. "We?"

Gaëlle snorted. "I don't have the time to play games, Eli. You know you're as curious about this as me. If we're going into that house tonight, we have some planning to do. Your place or mine?"

Before Eli could notice the blush in her cheeks, Gaëlle jumped off her chair and almost ran toward the exit. She didn't even turn to see what he'd do.

She knew he'd follow.

Five

At three in the morning, they slipped out of the Wilted Horseshoe. Gaëlle was relieved to see the old man was no longer in his chair, so he was probably not dead. To Gaëlle's inner clock, it was noon so she was ready to have some adventure, but Eli was having more trouble. He'd fallen asleep on Gaëlle's bed around midnight, leaving Gaëlle to finish their planning alone.

That was all right, she did her best work alone. Besides, he looked cute sleeping with his mouth hanging open and jerking awake from his own snores every twenty minutes.

Now he led the way through Cave Creek, choosing the darkest streets and keeping away from the shops with CCTVs. He only stopped twice because he was yawning so hard he couldn't see where he was going.

"This is it," he whispered and touched the back wall of one of four houses in a dark alley. "The back of Beau's house. Their back yard was over that fence over there. You got the grapple hook?"

Gaëlle did her best not to giggle at having someone say that in real life. With access to Eli's tool shed, they'd prepared a whole bunch of fun stuff for their expedition. She handed the grapple to Eli.

Who went ahead and hooked it perfectly on the eaves two floors up on the first try.

"I worked summers on my uncle's ranch when I was younger." He flashed a cocky grin, then scaled up the wall like some cowboy version of Spiderman.

Once he got the window up there forced open, he threw down a knotted rope to Gaëlle, helping her climb up to join him.

Gaëlle hadn't realized something could smell abandoned. But this house definitely did. Like no living being had breathed here in years. None of the usual background sounds of a lived-in house were present. No air-conditioning humming, no refrigerator firing up, no ticking clocks. A thick layer of dust covered everything in the bedroom they had entered, putting a damper not only on the colors, but also the echos of their steps as they crossed toward the door. They were leaving a trail so obvious a half-blind grandma would be able to spot it, but that didn't really matter. They weren't staying long.

Gaëlle activated the camera she had strapped to her front. This equipment wasn't from Eli's shed but from her own suitcase. She didn't only want to prove to herself her mom wasn't a witch—she needed proof to show her dad.

Eli led the way as they went through every room upstairs. They found three bedrooms. One parental suite, one that had probably been Beau's, judging by the faded football posters and nineties men's clothes lying scattered across the bed, and one that must have been a guest bedroom. Two bathrooms and one closet.

Nothing explaining where Beau had disappeared to. No obvious link to the Chamber of Commerce. And no listing of sports results of the future.

The old staircase creaked alarmingly as they made their way downstairs in silence. Gaëlle had lots of observations pop into her head as they explored but it didn't feel right to give them voice. This place felt like a tomb and a memorial, and she didn't want to disrupt it more than they were already doing.

Downstairs, things started to feel off. At first Gaëlle couldn't figure out why.

"They spent all their time in the kitchen," Eli stated, a frown marring his forehead and his hands on his hips as he stood by the front door looking back and forth between the kitchen area on his right and the living room area on his left.

Yep, that was the problem, all right.

The living room had a couch, an old TV, bookshelves…all the normal stuff. But except for the thick layer of dust, the couch looked pristine like it had never been in use.

The couch in the kitchen—who puts a couch in their kitchen?—was well-worn and coming off at the seams. Its back was to the cooking area, making it face…an empty wall.

"We knew this family was weird," Eli mumbled as he walked

over to knock on the wall. It sounded hollow. "But spending your life staring at a wall is pushing it, even for them."

Gaëlle glanced over at the living room. "That wall is hiding something. The house doesn't stop there."

Eli sighed. "Of course. It's a dry-wall with a hiding space." He started running his fingers along the sides. Tapped his fingers in several places, indicating where he found irregularities. "It shouldn't take too long to dismount at least part of it. I'm not sure we brought enough tools to get it back up and looking the same, though."

Gaëlle dragged a finger through the dust on the kitchen counter. "I'm not sure anyone will notice in the next decade."

They got to work, removing the plaster covering up the screws for the central-most pane and unscrewing all the attachments. Thirty minutes later, at about four in the morning, they carefully eased the drywall free and set it aside.

Oddly enough, there seemed to be sunlight pouring out from behind the wall.

"*Oh, putain,*" Gaëlle whispered.

"That a version of 'oh fuck' in French?" Eli whispered back. Neither of them moved a muscle.

"Yeah."

They were looking into a mirror. Sort of.

They were definitely seeing this same kitchen—same counter, same cabinets, same window—but it was daytime. And there was no dust.

And a guy in his thirties sipping coffee at the counter, while reading a newspaper.

"That's Beau." Eli's whisper was so low Gaëlle could barely hear it. The guy with the coffee didn't react.

"Wouldn't he be in his late fifties today?" Gaëlle asked.

"That's the Beau I've seen pictures of," Eli insists, his face suddenly very pale, "but about ten years older than when he disappeared."

"Maybe he had a brother."

Eli emitted what could only be qualified as a squeak. "He didn't. But I'll let that slide and state the even more obvious. It's clearly early morning where he's sitting."

"It's a huge-ass screen!" Gaëlle yelled, confident she'd found the solution. "They somehow filmed themselves and then sat here, watching…themselves." Weird, but not *as* weird as the alternatives.

Eli cringed when Gaëlle spoke, clearly ready to run them both off to safety if the Beau in the picture gave any indication of hearing them.

He didn't. He kept sipping his coffee and turned a page on his newspaper.

Gaëlle took one step closer so she stood where the drywall had been.

Beau looked up. Saw her. Eyebrows shot up in surprise—

And the view shifted.

The same house, but under construction. The kitchen was nothing put pipes protruding from the floor. No Beau. Afternoon sunlight coming in from the opposite direction of just seconds earlier.

"That's actual sunlight," Eli said, now standing shoulder-to-shoulder with Gaëlle. "No TV screen knows how to do that. See how it falls on that red line on the floor there?"

Gaëlle wouldn't have thought it possible, but her mouth went even dryer. That *was* real sunlight. And not only was the time of day different on the other side, it was a different temperature. She could feel waves of heat hitting her face, making goosebumps stand up on her arms. The smell of coffee she hadn't realized was there in the first scene faded.

"It's a portal." Eli points toward the ceiling. "See the edge up there? And around on both sides… I'd say it's a complete circle, with part of it under the floor. That is *not* a TV screen."

Gaëlle wondered if her camera was still recording. Would she ever be able to show this to anyone? Would anyone believe her?

She took a step toward the bright kitchen, only to have Eli pull her back.

"Do *not* go through that thing. We don't know how it works. It might be dangerous. Beau and his mother both *disappeared* from this house, remember?"

"I won't touch it," Gaëlle promised. "But I want to explore."

The space between the drywall and the screen/portal/whatever was about three meters wide. A thick, red line had been painted about one step in front of where it cut through the floor and it had "DANGER" written across it. Gaëlle would heed the warning.

It seemed like the portal stood against the back wall of the house. She couldn't see anything behind it, and wasn't willing to risk stepping across the line, not yet anyway. The rest was just empty space.

The image shifted again.

Same place. Different time. Early evening, by the looks of it.

And a family sitting down for dinner.

"That's Beau and his father." Eli gulped. "And his mother."

The Beau in the image before them was no more than fifteen, but there was no doubt about it being the younger version of the coffee drinker from earlier. He was rocking his chair back on its hind legs and his mother was scolding him for it.

Like before, the temperature changed as air flowed from the image. But there was no sound. They also hadn't reacted to Eli speaking, so it seemed fair to conclude it went both ways.

Then the father looked up. Straight at Gaëlle.

A frown. A quick glance above Gaëlle's head. He said something to his wife, and the three of them turned to stare.

"It says September 1990 on their calendar," Eli says.

Indeed, in a prominent spot next to the window, there was a calendar with writing so big it could easily be read from across the room. The clock hanging beside it claimed it was seven o'clock.

Gaëlle whipped her head around to look up at the back of the drywall, where the father had glanced.

A digital clock, giving the time and date. Including the year.

"It opens on the same space but at different times," she said in awe.

"Actually," a voice said from behind them, "it's different timelines. Martha had already stepped out of ours by that time."

Gaëlle and Eli both whirled around to face the new arrival, but not before seeing the relief on the three faces on the other side of the portal.

"Cole," Eli said. "What's going on here? Has the Chamber of Commerce been keeping this a secret for all these years?"

The man must be in his late seventies. He had sparse white hair sticking out from under a black fedora, a white shirt with the buttons done up skewed, and a pair of jeans with white sneakers.

He pointed to Gaëlle's chest. "I'm gonna have to ask you to turn that off, hon, and give me the camera so I can erase it."

"Cole," Eli started, "you can't just barge in here—"

"People are watching us on camera right now, young man. If you don't comply, more people will come, and we *will* end up getting what we need from you. It is to protect Cave Creek." He nodded to the family of three who were still watching from their kitchen. "And to protect them. We've yet to meet a line we won't cross to ensure that protection."

Gaëlle was quickly gaining an understanding of why her mother had been so scared when she'd used her knowledge of the future to place that bet. These Chamber of Commerce people must have scared her big time to exact the promise she wouldn't abuse or share the information. On the surface, Cole looked like a sweet grandfatherly type, but there was a hard edge to him. One Gaëlle didn't want to run up against.

She unhooked the camera from her shirt and handed it over. "Do what you need," she said. "I came for answers and I guess I have them."

Cole accepted the camera with a nod. "You can't tell anyone what you saw here, hon. I suppose your mother is Eléonore? You look just like her."

Gaëlle nodded numbly. "Can't I please just tell my dad? He thinks my mom is a witch." Her voice broke on the last word.

"I'm afraid not, hon. Especially if he has *those* kind of tendencies. He'd tell the world our secret and we'd lose Cave Creek as we know it."

"What happened to Beau?" Eli asked. Behind them, the scene had changed again. An old lady was doing the dishes while surrounded by fancy-looking appliances. The digital calendar on the wall read 2029.

"This house has been in their family since it was built not long after the founding of Cave Creek. The portal was the family secret. Their view into future descendants they'd never meet, a look at old memories, or could-have-beens. They warned each other of disasters to avoid, and gave each other some information that could be used for financial gain in a pinch. Beau, unfortunately, ignored that last bit when he found himself alone.

"The particularity of this portal is that it's one way. You don't just go through, see? You bounce back to the exact spot you were at. Like a mirror. So if you go through, you can't come back. Unless it opens back into the same timeline later, but in the fourteen years Beau's father sat here waiting, it never happened. We haven't figured out the logic to the time jumps in this one yet."

The scene shifted again, and this time it seemed to be an actual mirror. The back of a boarded-up wall, with a digital calendar—ah, slightly off, it was two years in the future—and a big sign on the central part: "Nobody left, do not come through."

"The drywall you removed has the same sign," Cole said, his voice sombre. "Beau's dad believed his wife stepped through one day because the Beau on the other side needed help. He wanted to follow her, and waited for years to find her again. Beau... He didn't handle being alone very well. And when his thoughtless actions here caught up with him, he stepped through to sometime else. We don't know where, only hope it was a version where he could be with his family again."

Gaëlle noted him saying "*this* portal," meaning there were others. But she wanted to make sure she would be allowed to leave this place and go home, and knowing as little as possible was clearly the best way to go.

"So how do I get my dad off my mom's back?" she asked. "I assume you have experience with this stuff?"

"Tell her to get away while she still can." Cole's voice was hard, unyielding. "If he doesn't trust her now, he never will. Can I count on your discretion? Eléonore has shown we were right to trust *her* when she left Cave Creek."

Gaëlle didn't need to think about her answer. "I'll keep your secret." And the man was probably right. Telling her dad there were portals to other timelines in a town in Nevada wouldn't get him to believe his wife. It would probably just turn him against his daughter as well.

"And you, Eli," Cole said, squaring his shoulders as he stared down the younger man. "I think it's time you came to a Chamber of Commerce meeting. The important ones. That Bed & Breakfast of yours seems to be working out quite well. You need to be part of our community and help us protect our secret from the outside world."

Gaëlle held back a laugh as Eli's chest puffed out with pride. "I guess I could come to one meeting, at least. As long as it's not illegal or anything?"

"We do what we must to protect our town," Cole replied, making a chill go down Gaëlle's spine. "But the more of us there are, the easier it is find easy solutions—like today. If we hadn't had a security camera on the portal, who knows what you would have done."

Gaëlle glanced over her shoulder at the portal—which showed nothing but barren land and the mountains in the distance. Either *way* into the future or to a point in the past where the house wasn't built yet.

She'd leave the people of Cave Creek to protect their town. She would focus on protecting her mother.

In a way, her plan hadn't changed at all.

AUTHOR'S NOTE

THANK YOU FOR reading *Moneyline Secrets*. I hope you enjoyed it!

This story was written for, and first published in, the Cave Creek anthology, *Open Ended Threat*. This anthology contains stories set in the present, written by lots of talented writers, so make sure to check it out.

I have a second story set around the same portal and family. It's turning into a series. The story is called *Family Secrets*. This one was part of the *Bitter Mountain Moonlight* anthology, the one set in the past.

There's bound to be more stories in this series, so if you like it, make sure you sign up for my newsletter, to make sure you're up to speed on all new publications.

By signing up for my newsletter, you'll also get several free stories, for example the first Ghost Detective short story, *Just Desserts*.

R.W. Wallace
www.rwwallace.com

ABOUT THE AUTHOR

R.W. Wallace writes in most genres, though she tends to end up in mystery more often than not. Dead bodies keep popping up all over the place whenever she sits down in front of her keyboard.

The stories mostly take place in Norway or France; the country she was born in and the one that has been her home for two decades. Don't ask her why she writes in English—she won't have a sensible answer for you.

Her Ghost Detective short story series appears in *Pulphouse Magazine*, starting in issue #9.

You can find all her books, long and short, all genres, on rwwallace.com.

Also by R.W. Wallace

Mystery

Ghost Detective Novels
Beyond the Grave
Unveiling the Past
Beneath the Surface

Ghost Detective Shorts
Just Desserts
Lost Friends
Family Bonds
Common Ground
Till Death
Family History
Heritage
Eternal Bond
New Beginnings
Severed Ties

The Tolosa Mystery Series
The Red Brick Haze
The Red Brick Cellars
The Red Brick Basilica

Short Story Collections
Deep Dark Secrets
A Thief in the Night

Short Stories
Cold Blue Eternity
Hidden Horrors

Critters
Gertrude and the Trojan Horse
First Impressions
Let Them Eat Cake
Out of Sight
Sitting Duck
Two's Company
Like Mother Like Daughter

Time Travel Secrets (short stories)

Moneyline Secrets
Family Secrets

Romance

French Office Romance Series

Flirting in Plain Sight
Hiding in Plain Sight
Loving in Plain Sight

Short Stories

Down the Memory Aisle

Holiday Short Stories

Morbier Impossible
A Second Chance
The Magic of Sharing
The Case of the Disappearing Gingerbread City
The Lucia Crown

Young Adult (short stories)

Unexpected Consequences
The Art of Pretending
First Impressions

www.ingramcontent.com/pod-product-compliance
Lightning Source LLC
LaVergne TN
LVHW041600070526
838199LV00046B/2071